Joan Vegas

FOOLED-PLEASURED -PLEASED

One Wife's Report on being introduced to the pleasures of New Guy Sex

WARNING

This book contains sexually explicit scenes and adult language. It may be considered offensive to some readers. This book is for sale to adults ONLY.

* * * * * * * * * * * * * * * * * * *

Please store your files wisely where they cannot be accessed by underage readers.

Please feel free to send me an email. Just know that these emails are filtered by my publisher. Good news is always welcome.

Joan Vegas - **joan_vegas@awesomeauthors.org**

You might also want to check my blog for Updates and interesting info.
http://joan-vegas.awesomeauthors.org/

About the Publisher

4Fun Publishing, a member of **BLVNP Incorporated,** 340 S. Lemon #6200, Walnut CA 91789, info@blvnp.com / legal@blvnp.com
NOTE: Due to the highly emotional reaction of some people to works of erotic fiction, any email sent to the above address that contains foul language or religious references is automatically deleted by our anti-spam software and will not be seen. All other communications are welcome.

DISCLAIMER

Please don't be stupid and kill yourself. This book is a work of FICTION. Do not try any new sexual practice that you find in this book. It is fiction and not to be confused with reality. Neither the author nor the publisher or its associates assume any responsibility for any loss, injury, death or legal consequences resulting from acting on the contents in this book. Every character in this book is over 18 years of age. The author's opinions are not to be construed as the opinions of the publisher. The material in this book is for entertainment purposes ONLY. Enjoy.

Fooled – Pleasured - Pleased
One Wife's Report on being introduced
To the pleasures of New Guy Sex

By: Joan Vegas

© Joan Vegas 2013
ISBN: 978-1-62761-678-2

I am writing because I became aware of your web site and its advice or reports about couples who have experienced MFM threesomes. You are welcome to share my letter with others.

A little background: I am now 38-years-old and have been married to my husband Mel for 11 years. What I am about to tell you started two years ago. We live in Indiana. My husband is a real estate agent and I work part-time as a secretary in an insurance office. We have one son who is now 9.

Immediately after our son was born I got on birth control pills, not wanting to get pregnant again too soon. Then about two years later Mel and I decided one child was enough, so I have stayed on the pill ever since.

My husband and I have what I believe is a very good, mutually-respectful, and loving marriage. We started having sex before we were married, as many couples do. Prior to that I had only had sex with two other guys... Mel had experienced sex with at least a half dozen women before we met. Until what I am about to tell you happened... neither of us had any outside affairs, etc.

My husband tells me I should describe myself. For what it is worth, I stand 5' 3", typically weigh about 125 (I think I am overweight), have C-36 boobs, blonde hair and blue eyes. I exercise regularly, and my husband tells me I am "cute". Oh, by the way, I tend to be multi-orgasmic. Nice huh!

My husband keeps himself in shape too (he is one year my senior), and is always very loving. I think he is a handsome man and an excellent lover.

From the earliest days of our relationship Mel has always been very inventive in our sex play. He would occasionally stop at the video rental shop and bring home adult videos for us to watch while the two of us were alone. Then after a while he would stop at the adult shop and pick up magazines and sex toys. I always got a kick out of the stuff he brought home.

We played with the dildos and vibrators as we had sex. Sometimes Mel would con me into going out in the evening without panties under my dresses. It's not that we tried any exhibitionism, etc., he just liked the idea that he could play with me as we drove to and from our night-out destinations. I kind'a liked that too.

One time, he and I took a weekend trip to Chicago. We stayed at the Palmer House in downtown Chicago so we could attend a play there. That was one of the nights he convinced me to leave my panties back at the hotel room. I wore a rather demure dress that night, but during the play (while it was fairly dark) I felt Mel's hand work its way under my dress and up toward my crotch.

I decided to let him have his fun since I was sure no one could see what he was doing. I spread my legs a bit and felt him begin to tickle my clit. It felt good, but… fearing I might start wiggling around or make unintended pleasure sounds as I approached orgasm… I brushed his hand away while grinning at him.

When we got back to the Palmer House we decided to wander around the convention area. By that hour no one was around. We found a large room where a convention dinner must have been held earlier in the evening. Most of the lights were still on. The dishes had all been cleared away, but all the table cloths and many of the napkins were still scattered on the tables.

Alone in the big room, Mel wrapped his arms around me and gave me a passionate kiss. Soon I felt his hands pulling up my dress from behind. I pulled away from our kiss and said, "Mel, what are you doing?" He replied, "I want to finish what I started in the theater." Having said that he resumed his kissing of my neck, face and lips as he moved me back against the end of one of the tables.

Even though the room was well lighted and I thought that someone could come in at any moment... I thought 'What the heck', and stopped resisting. He laid me back on the table, lifted the front of my dress, and began to diddle me as he grinned at me. I closed my eyes and enjoyed what he was doing.

Still lying on my back on the table, soon I felt his face at my crotch. He licked and nibbled on me until a most enjoyable orgasm overtook me. I tried to keep my moans of pleasure low. By the time I regained my senses I discovered that my husband had unzipped his pants and had his fully erect penis in his hand.

I started to rise from my position (lying on the table with my feet dangling off the end). Instead, Mel grabbed my legs, lifted them over his shoulders (causing me to fall back onto the table), and promptly inserted his hard penis into me. I was again aware of our semi-public location and my fully exposed bottom. Mel, standing at the end of the table) began a steady rhythm pumping in and out of me until the good sensations overtook my mind and I began to pump back against his thrusts.

Gawd that felt good... and naughty. As I watched my husband's face I knew it would not be long before he filled me. I just closed my eyes and enjoyed our coupling. Mel pumped me long enough and hard enough that I had another (more intense) orgasm just as I felt him squirt into me.

After a moment to recover I reached out and grabbed one of the cloth napkins that had been left on the table. I put it between my legs to keep Mel's nut juices from flowing down my legs as I rose to my feet. My dress fell into place. I looked around. No one had caught us. We both just started laughing as we headed for the door.

By the time we reached our room we were still both giggling about what we had just done. Before entering our room I reached between my legs and removed my temporary "sanitary napkin" and threw it onto a discarded food tray that was sitting in the hallway.

After shedding our clothes we flopped on the bed and had another round of great sex before falling asleep. Every once and a while we still talk about our night in the convention hall of the Parker House. And I admit that it was great fun.

We have also shared sex play on secluded beaches and in the back seat of our car at drive-in movies. So we have been sexually adventurous during our marriage... but always just the two of us until....

Mel continued to periodically bring home toys and sexy lingerie from various adult stores he ran across in his journeys. One time about three years ago he brought home a pair of fluffy soft handcuffs. They had Velcro tape to hold them in place. He had also purchased a couple of tie-down straps (the kind used to secure things in the back of pick-up trucks).

When I got out of the shower that evening in preparation for going to bed I discovered that Mel had stretched the tie-down straps under our king bed and connected them to the new handcuffs.

"What's this all about?" I asked. Grinning like a little boy with a new toy he said, "Lay in the middle of the bed, on your back, with your arms outstretched." Not wanting to spoil his boyish fun, I did as he had asked. I was still nude from the shower, as was he, and he dimmed the lights.

Once, he had each of the cuffs secured on my wrists he snugged the tie-down straps so that I was firmly (but gently) restrained... arms stretched toward the sides of our bed. Then he began kissing me all over my body. It felt good so I just relaxed and enjoyed our new form of play.

Mel worked his way down my body until his tongue was deeply embedded in my pussy. He spent a lot of time eating me. It felt sooo good! By the way, we always make a practice of showering before going to bed, to assure we are fresh for each other. I must have had 4 or 5 climaxes as he used his mouth on my pussy and clit… each more intense than the last. Then he climbed on top of me, entered me, and pumped me until I felt his penis expand… just before I felt his nut juice squirt within me.

A few more kisses while I was still restrained, and then he undid the cuffs before we cuddled and both fell asleep. It had been a fun new game. I genuinely enjoyed it. The next morning I just kicked the cuffs and tie-down straps under the bed as I made it, just in case my mother came over for a visit.

We used the cuffs a few nights a week over the next several months. Often, while I was gently restrained, Mel would use one of our vibrators on my pussy, or stuff if with one of the dildos he had purchased.

One night, while I was restrained, Mel kiddingly told me that some night he was going to bring a group of motorcycle bikers to our bedroom "to see, enjoy, and ravage your naked body" while you are restrained. "Not funny," I firmly told him. But he replied, "Well… not a group… but I think it would be a kick to see another guy fill your pussy and give you pleasure." I didn't comment.

That proved to be the first of numerous times during our love-making that Mel would mention his fantasy of seeing some other man have sex with me. The adult videos he brought home during that time tended to show two guys having sex with one gal. He also brought home magazines that featured stories of two-man – one-woman sex situations. We read them together, but I never expressed any interest in such sex play.

As a matter of fact I always told Mel that I could never see myself letting another man have sex with me. I told him I just wanted him… he was enough for me. I was firm about rejecting the idea of having another man in our marital bed, but underneath I did find the idea stimulating.

Often as we screwed at night Mel would still talk to me about what it would feel like to have a new penis playing within me. He would tell me he would love to see another man's "dick" slide in and out of me. Typically I just ignored his comments. But his words did cause me to have more intense orgasms. Still, I would not acknowledge any interest in the word pictures he was painting.

Then a little over two years ago Mel brought home a new sex toy… a combination sleep mask/blindfold. That night while he had me restrained and was eating me he brought out the new toy. He showed it to me, telling me he wanted me to be deprived of vision to enhance my focus on the pleasuring sensations he was giving to my pussy. He put it on me and tied it tightly. I could not see anything… not even any light from the edges.

He was right, being deprived of sight allowed me to focus more intently on the pleasure he was giving me with his mouth, tongue and fingers. I found that I liked it. However, I also became more verbal as I reached peaks of pleasure. As a result we limited that kind of play to nights when our son was visiting his grandparents. That way I could let louse my expressions of pleasure without wakening our son.

On about the third night that we shared this new blindfold game Mel had treated me to a couple orgasms with his mouth before he pulled away and said, "Now I'm going to let 'Fred' bury his dick in your pussy and make you feel good." I felt a body return between my legs, obviously kneeling at the end of the bed… as Mel often did. I felt my legs being lifted into the air and bed movement signaling kneeling on the bed between my legs. A hard penis made its way between the folds of my labia… and into my pussy.

The penis just rested inside me, all the way in. I could feel legs and balls pressed against me. "Mel,": I said… hesitantly… "that is you, isn't it?" No reply. Then I felt a pair of hands grab my breasts and begin to play with them. That's when the penis within me began to pump me quite vigorously. Again I said. "Mel… is that you?" Again, no response.

My mind was in a whirl, but my pussy was enjoying the sensations. Almost involuntarily my body convulsed in an orgasm. Then I felt nut juices flood me before my legs were allowed to drop down. The body apparently backed away from me and I heard my husband whisper, ":Good job Fred. You can go now."

Moments later Mel laid down next to me and gave me a kiss. "Did you enjoy that babe?" he asked as he released my cuffs and began to remove my blindfold?

"What did you do?" I asked incredulously. "Did you really have some other guy in here? And let him screw me?" He just smiled. That's about the time I felt that his penis was coated with my fresh pussy juices. I also realized that I had not heard our squeaky bedroom door open and close to let someone in and out. It was still closed.

"You rat!" I told my husband. "You made me think I was having sex with another man." He just grinned at me and refrained from admitting anything.

I had to admit that my husband's little game of deception had been fun. The experience even made me re-think my repeated objections to having sex with someone other than my husband... but I never admitted that to Mel.

The combination handcuff/blindfold games became a regular part of our shared sex play every time our son visited his grandparents. Mel even purchased another pair of tie-downs. He used the extra tie-downs around my knees, with my legs in the air. He connected the hook ends to my wrist cuffs... causing my legs to be held in the air, spread apart... so he didn't have to use his hands to hold them up as he treated me to oral sex. Sometimes Mel made no effort to play that another guy was in the room, and other times he did.

One night, while playing our little game (with my arms restrained and my legs held in the air by Mel's most recent invention) I sensed that the oral sex I was receiving somehow felt a bit different. 'Had my husband learned some new techniques?' I thought. I felt warm breath blow over my pubic area and then lavish tongue swirls around my pussy and clit… then quick tongue darts in and out of my pussy. The new kind of oral treats felt good.

Then, his full mouth sucked my clit and I felt teeth gently nibble on it. That sent me over the top, and I moaned quite loudly. I remember yelling, "Oh Hon, that felt so good." Then I felt his hard penis separate my pussy lips and press deeply into me. He held it deep inside, somehow making its head vibrate a little against my cervix. That felt good. Then he started pumping… pumping faster and harder than I had remembered my husband doing before.

I reached two more climaxes before I felt him expand and spray my insides. That wonderful sensation took me over the top yet again, leaving my head foggy for a few minutes. Yes, I heard a little rustling, but I didn't think anything of it   I had enjoyed a really good orgasm and was coming down from my "high" when I felt Mel crawl into bed and begin to cuddle with me.

On a night two weeks later, we played our game again. That time I sensed unfamiliar cologne. I even asked, "Hon, did you buy some new cologne?" As usual, he did not reply. My husband (I think) had already treated me to some great oral sex, and by then the penis within me was feeling extra good… driving me to an enjoyable climax. Hands were cupping and fondling my breasts.

I think I was again extra loud with my moans of pleasure that night. I could not believe how long the penis within me stayed hard and continued to work me through repeated and intense orgasms. I began to think Mel had gotten hold of some Viagra. The extended sex had felt extra good.

But, I noticed that the penis within me was still hard, and had not climaxed... in spite of its extended play within me. Yet it pulled out. I heard some rustling, and then my Mel was again cuddling me. To be honest, during our games I often thought it might be interesting if Mel snuck some other guy into our bedroom (I didn't know he had oiled our squeaking door) and had twice let unseen, unknown guys actually screw me... but I never really believed he would do it.

That time, once he released my handcuffs, I reached over and felt my husband's penis. It was soft and dry! As he removed my blindfold I looked Mel directly in his eyes and asked "Who was that?" He said, "What do you mean?" I shook his soft penis and said, "This dry penis did not just come out of me!"

Caught, Mel rolled onto his back and remained quiet. Finally, rather than answering my question, he asked, "Did you enjoy it?" "That really was some other guy... wasn't it," I asked. He repeated his question... "Did you enjoy it?"

I could see I wasn't going to get an answer to my question until I answered his. I laid back, rested for a moment, and finally said, "Yes... but who was it?" Rising up on his elbow my husband said, "I'm glad you enjoyed it. Your moans certainly told me you were enjoying it."

"OK smarty," I replied, "I still want to know who you just let have sex with me."

Mel hesitated a bit and finally said, "You don't know him and other than tonight, he doesn't know you." "How did you meet him," I demanded. "Through an ad on CraigsList", he finally admitted.

"You mean you just met some guy on-line and invited him over to screw me," I asked, somewhat angrily. "No," he replied, "met him several times, got to know him, and finally arranged for him to come over tonight."

"How about the other times that we played our little handcuff/blindfold game? Did you have other guys do me those times too?" I asked. "Only once babe," he replied. "Two weeks ago it was another guy… again someone you don't know. I met and got to know him through CraigsList too."

We were both quiet for several minutes. Finally Mel said, "It was really cool watching their dicks enter and fill you. I had a hard time remaining quite. I watched your body respond both times, and I'm pretty sure you liked the feeling of them play within you." I didn't respond. Mel kissed me, wrapped his arms around me and said, "I love you very much babe, and again I must say it was cool watching your body respond to those new dicks within you." Again I didn't say anything,

We cuddled and finally fell asleep in each other's arms. The next morning (a Saturday) I had coffee and breakfast ready for Mel when he came down. As we drank coffee I confronted my husband with my feelings. I told him I felt deceived… or at least fooled by what he had done. Then I surprised him by telling him I wanted to meet the two guys who had had sex with me. "You owe me at least that much", I told him. "They have seen me… totally nude… and gotten to know me intimately. I need to at least know what they look like."

Mel was clearly surprised by my request. Yet, he seemed pleased that I wasn't really pissed. He agreed to set up a meeting at a local lounge.

To my surprise, an hour later he told me we were going to meet "Sheldon" for drinks that evening. He explained that "Sheldon" was the first guy… the one who had treated me to the extra enjoyable oral sex before entering me and filling me with his juices.

I don't think I was quite prepared for such a quick meeting. I spent the rest of the day fussing around and picking out the clothes I would wear that night. I knew "Sheldon" had already seen me nude, but I wanted to show myself dressed up as a proper lady.

Mel led me to a booth in the far corner, away from where others might hear our conversation. Even before a waitress came over to take our order, this attractive younger good looking man approached our table. Mel stood up and said "Hi Sheldon, glad you could join us." The young man returned Mel's greeting before smiling at me and saying, "Hi, I'm Sheldon."

He politely extended his hand toward me, so I accepted his hand and politely shook it. I felt like I had to say something, so I said, "I'm pleased to meet you." Mel patted the seat next to him, encouraging Sheldon to sit down. He did, just as the waitress walked up.

We each ordered a drink, and the waitress walked away. There was silence for a few pregnant moments. Finally I said, "Well Sheldon, I understand you were over at our home a couple weeks ago… while I was in bed!" Sheldon looked at Mel, then back at me.

"Yes, you were in bed when I visited your home," he replied. "And nude," I added to his acknowledgement. He shook his head affirmatively. "And blindfolded… and restrained," I went on. "That's true," he said, with a broad smile on his face.

"I believe you had sex with me too," I went on, "after using your mouth on my pussy." There was a pause as the two guys looked at each other. Finally Sheldon said, "I confess… that was me. I hope I gave you pleasure. That was my objective."

Then I went silent… thinking back on that night and the good sensations I had enjoyed. "You know," I said, "I was pretty pissed at my husband when I learned that he had deceived and fooled me… but, yes, you did give me pleasure."

Sheldon reached across the table and put his hand on mine while saying, "I'm sorry you were pissed at our fooling you, but your husband told me he wanted you to experience sex with another guy as he watched, and when I arrived in your bedroom I found you so beautiful and sexy that I wanted to fulfill his wish while giving you my best."

I blushed at his "beautiful and sexy" words. All I could think of to say was, "You sure know how to use your mouth and tongue to turn a woman on." The two guys smiled at my comments. About then our drinks arrived.

Over the drinks, we made small talk. I learned that Sheldon was 29, divorced, and had two kids. He said he has a regular girlfriend. I asked if she knew he had had sex with another woman. He admitted that she did not... that he had responded to Mel's ad so that he too could experience sex with someone other than his long-term girlfriend. He assured me he had really enjoyed the experience, and hoped someday to introduce his girlfriend to sex with another guy.

As we finished our drinks Sheldon told us he had to leave so he could get home to his girlfriend. He reached for my hand again, squeezed it, and said, "I hope you enjoyed our 'connection' as much as I did... and if you are ever open to doing it again without blindfold and restraints, I hope you will have Mel contact me." I just smiled.

After Sheldon threw down a few bucks for his drink, said goodbye to both of us, and left... Mel said, "Well, what do you think of Sheldon?" I wasn't about to give him a ringing endorsement of the man he had used to fool me, but I did say, "He seems nice... clean cut. Actually he is kind of handsome. I'm glad you didn't just pick some dirty old man."

I hadn't noticed that a single guy had entered the lounge, was sitting at the bar. Mel pointed him out to me. "That's Reggie," he informed me, "your lover from last night." "Seriously?" I exclaimed, "I'm going to meet both men on the same night?"

Mel told me he had contacted Reggie about meeting us, but did not know if he was going to be able to come. I noticed that "Reggie" didn't make any move to join us. He was apparently waiting for Mel to beckon to him. "Would you like to meet him?" Mel asked. "I might just as well," I replied, "and get to know both guys who had sex with me all at one time." I went on to mutter, "That sounds really weird!"

Mel beckoned to "Reggie". The man, I judged to be a couple years older than me, began to walk over toward us. He smiled at both of us, said "Hi" to Mel, and slid in next to me while sitting his drink on our table. He looked at me and said, "You're just as pretty dressed as you were last night when I saw you nude. But now that I can see your face… you're even cuter than I thought."

What an awkward moment. I sensed the aroma of the cologne I had smelled the night before. There I was sitting next to a man who had had sex with me less than 24 hours before… yet he was a man I had never met. I looked at Mel. He was grinning. Then I looked back at the smiling Reggie. I managed to say, "Nice to meet you."

I began to warm up to Reggie as the three of us talked. I asked him if he did to other wives what he had done the previous night to me. He replied, "Yes and no. No I have never before done that with a woman who was blindfolded and partly restrained. But, yes, I have occasionally joined husbands who wanted to double their wife's pleasure." His answer surprised me a bit.

Finally I asked him the question I had on my mind ever since the previous evening. "I noticed that you were able to maintain your erection for a long time, and you gave me several orgasms… yet you didn't seem to have an orgasm of your own."

Reggie put his hand on my shoulder and told me that was part of his deal with Mel. He said, "I promised to focus all my energy on giving you pleasure. I just happen to be blessed with the capacity to screw for a long time. By the time I was sure you had enjoyed several climaxes it was clear you were tired. So I decided to forego my own climax… in hopes there would be another opportunity with you." His comments left my mind in a whirl! 'Another opportunity with me?' I thought. I didn't say anything.

Both Mel and Reggie were looking at me. I guess they hoped I would say something. I remained silent as I took a sip of my drink.

"You DID enjoy Reggie's play on and in your body… didn't you babe?" my husband finally said. Again I remained silent. Reggie spoke up and said, "The reactions of your body sure made me think you were enjoying what I was doing. I would be disappointed if I failed to give you pleasure."

I looked at him, with a slight smile on my face, and admitted, "Yes… I did enjoy the pleasure you gave me, even though I really thought it was my husband inside me." Moments later I went on to tell them both that the previous night I had experienced some extra enjoyable, extended orgasms.

"Good," said Reggie, "and now I must be going so I can leave you two alone to discuss your newly expanded sex life. He gave me a light peck of a kiss on my forehead, shook Mel's hand, and left us.

Mel and I just sort of looked at each other, finished our drinks and left. When we got home we took our showers and went right to bed. Mel cuddled with me. He gave me a passionate kiss while fondling my breasts. "They were both nice," I said. "I think you enjoyed the sex with both of them too," Mel whispered.

He began to stroke my pussy and clit. "I sure enjoyed watching both of them play with you babe. It was fun to watch Sheldon eat you so well, and to watch Reggie play inside you for so long," he said. I began to feel pleasant sensations between my legs as Mel said, "It was especially cool to watch their dicks part your pussy lips and disappear inside you. I had a hard time staying quiet."

By then my body was squirming. "I want YOU inside me," I blurted out. My husband was inside me and pumping in no time. It felt really good. I guess my libido was extra primed after meeting and talking with two men who had had sex with me.

As Mel pumped me toward orgasm he said, "Next time I want to hold you in my arms and neck with you as one of them pumps within you." I momentarily thought 'next time?' as Mel's play within me sent me over the top. As I climaxed I felt him release his nut juices... prolonging and intensifying my orgasm. We cuddled, and soon fell asleep.

The next morning, a Sunday, our son was still with his grandparents. We took advantage of that and slept in. When I awoke I looked up to see my husband leaning on one elbow, looking down at me with a broad smile on his face. "What?" I said. He just said, "My wife is extra beautiful when she is sexually fulfilled. I love you."

I told him I love him too, reached up, put my arms around his neck, drew him to me and gave him a good morning kiss. He laid back and I laid my head on his chest. Eventually I said, "Last night you said 'next time'... are you serious?" "I sure am babe... if you will allow me to give you that treat again."

I told him I wasn't sure about that. I reminded him that I had felt fooled and deceived. He promptly responded, "But you admitted that you enjoyed both guys... right?" I couldn't deny that. Instead I began fondling his penis. In no time it was hard and straight. We had sex again. Then it was time to shower and go get our son.

Over the next ten days Mel and I talked about Sheldon and Reggie and the unintended sex I had with them. I finally admitted to Mel that the experiences had been stimulating... that I had enjoyed them. He finally convinced me to try "other man sex" again with Reggie and/or Sheldon. "But," I insisted, "next time the blindfold and restraints have to go." I guess I was committing myself to a "next time".

To my surprise, the very next night Mel came home from work, took me in his arms, and announced, "It's all set up for Saturday night". I asked what was set up. He said he had already made plans for our son to spend the night with his parents, and he had made arrangements for Sheldon to visit us. 'Wow, that was fast', I thought... but I didn't object. I had already been thinking about the wonderful oral sex Sheldon had treated me to before.

Over the next two days, I could think of little other than Saturday night. I found myself floating between 'you shouldn't do this... it's crazy'... to 'well it really isn't cheating, Mel is setting it up'. Then more thoughts. 'Why would you voluntarily let a man other than your husband have sex with you?' to 'I did enjoy the way he licked and sucked me... and the later realization that it was not Mel gave me shivers of pleasure'.

Saturday evening finally rolled around. Mel took our son to his grandparents' home. After dinner Mel took a shower, came down in his robe, hugged me, and gave me a hot kiss. "I know you are going to enjoy tonight," he whispered. I just smiled and went upstairs for my shower.

Sheldon arrived while I was still in the shower. Before leaving the bathroom I put on a full-length white lacy gown that Mel had purchased for that evening... nothing else. I spritzed on some perfume. When I entered the room, I found Mel and Sheldon standing there waiting for me... nude... with big grins on their faces.

Mel reached out and undid the tie on my gown. Sheldon lifted it off my shoulders. I felt shudders go through my body. 'This is it,' I thought... without saying anything. Each taking one of my hands, they guided me to the bed. Mel dimmed the lights as Sheldon encouraged me to get on my back in the middle of the bed.

Quickly they were on the bed with me, Mel on one side and Sheldon on the other. I did not know what I was supposed to do, so I just laid there looking up. Sheldon, on his side facing me, began nuzzling my neck as he reached over and began playing with my nearest breast. Mel, also on his side facing me, reached over to turn my face toward him. He planted a gentle kiss on my lips while reaching for my other breast.

As they kissed me all over my neck, shoulders, and face... their hands roamed my nude body. I shivered from the pleasant sensations. I closed my eyes and began to relax as I enjoyed the feel of their touches, and their soft kisses.

Soon I felt Sheldon kiss his way down across my tummy. He got out of bed and I felt his hands begin to gently spread my legs. I knew what was coming. I think I was actually eager to feel his mouth on my private parts once again. He did not disappoint.

I felt his warm breath blow across my clit and pussy lips. Then, a gentle swipe of his tongue up between my pussy lips. It felt oh so good. Meanwhile Mel had moved up a bit on the bed, wrapped his arms around me, and drawn my head onto his chest. I knew he was watching Sheldon work his oral magic on my pussy.

Eyes once again closed, I focused my mental energies on the wonderful sensations between my legs. Mel had each of my breasts in his hands, cupping and gently squeezing them. I felt him plant a kiss on my forehead just as I felt Sheldon's tongue dart inside my vagina. What a unique sensation... being kissed on my forehead by my husband as another mouth gave me pleasure at my pussy!

I think both my mind and my body were being simultaneously stimulated by the situation and the pleasure-filled sensations. I felt a quiet orgasm build within me. It peaked without me letting out a moan. But a few minutes later, as Sheldon's tongue circled around within my pussy... playing on my G spot... I felt another climax beginning to build.

My body began to squirm a bit. I think Mel felt my movement. He squeezed my nipples while again kissing my forehead. That sent me over the top. That time I was not quiet. I let out a moan of pleasure that I am sure our son would have heard, had he been home in his room. The wonderful sensations at my crotch went on and on. My orgasm seemed to go on and on. Eventually I had to push Sheldon's head away. He again crawled up next to me.

Mel moved back down next to me again too. I heard Mel whisper in my ear, "I think you liked that. Am I right?" I shook my head affirmatively. Meanwhile Sheldon had moved his talented mouth to my nearest breast. He was sucking much of it deep into his mouth. I felt his tongue flick across my nipple. I shuddered.

Taking Sheldon's lead, Mel began sucking on my other breast. All the attention left me feeling well satisfied and mellow. By then I had reached for the cocks on either side of me. They were both hard. I wrapped my hands around both of them and gave them each a stroke.

I heard myself saying, "I really need to have one of you inside me." 'Did I really say that,' I thought. Sheldon wasted no time. He scurried down to the end of the bed, lifted my legs, and knelt on the bed between them. Meanwhile Mel had worked his way to the top of the bed, was leaning against the headboard, spread his legs, and drew me between his outstretched legs, and placed my head onto his lap. I felt his hard penis against my shoulder.

Mel reached over me and grasped my ankles, taking my legs from Sheldon. My knees were just above my breasts. I saw Sheldon smile at me as I felt the head of his penis begin to make its way between my pussy lips. He stopped a moment. "No blindfold this time. Are you OK?" he asked. By then I was eager to feel him inside me. "Yes… yes," I responded, "I want you inside me." Our eyes locked as he slowly pressed forward. My eyes closed as I savored the mental and physical stimulation of another man's penis beginning to play within me.

I knew that from his position against the headboard, holding my legs spread apart, my husband was watching Sheldon's penis enter and slowly pump me. I felt his upper body lean toward me. Then I heard him whisper, "What a beautiful picture… watching another guy's dick enter and explore you. I love you so much babe… and I want you to enjoy every sensation your femininity possesses. This is a scene I have long wanted to watch while holding you."

Sheldon picked up his pace. He drove deeply into me, pressing his public bone against my sensitive clit with each thrust. He reached up and took my breasts into his hands while running his thumb over my nipples. I was soon moaning again, enjoying the unorthodox screwing I was getting. I felt Sheldon's penis begin to expand inside me. The extra fullness sent me over the top. I bucked, pressed tightly against Sheldon's inward pumps, and began one long moan of satisfaction.

Then it hit. I felt Sheldon press extra tightly against me. He bent forward with his head between my upturned legs. His face told me he was on the brink of unloading his nut juice. As he let loose, an intense orgasm washed through me. He told me later that during his release my vagina contracted in a vibrating effect, causing him to have a most enjoyable climax.

Sheldon pulled out of me. He again laid on the bed beside me, but that time he laid face up, breathing deeply, recovering from our vigorous sex romp. Mel worked his way off the bed and made his way to the foot of the bed. He laid on top of me, missionary-style, and I felt his hard penis make its way inside me. "You are so slick and hot," he whispered to me. His face was close enough that he gave me a passionate kiss as his penis pumped within me. "What a feeling" he announced, "screwing my wife while she is well lubricated with another man's jizz. It feels amazing!"

As Mel pumped me, my capacity for pleasure returned. 'Wow,' I thought, 'two different penises screwing me within moments of each other.' Again, that mental stimulation, coupled with the renewed good feelings within my pussy… yet another orgasm began to build within me. I felt Sheldon lean over and kiss my cheek while my husband increased his pace. I turned my face toward Sheldon and gave him a full-on, tongue-dipping kiss as I grabbed his slick penis.

I know Mel was watching me kiss Sheldon. I think that sight enhanced my husband's pleasure. I felt him expand within me. I broke my kiss with Sheldon just as my husband and I shared nearly simultaneous orgasms. Mel returned to my side, lying on his back.

By then we were all three drained and breathing hard. We all rested quietly for several minutes. Then I heard myself say, "I can't believe I let myself do that!" It was Sheldon who turned to me and said, "I'll bet you're glad you did. I know I sure am." Then I heard Mel chime in, "I am too".

Joan, memories of that first night of knowingly having sex with another man gives me great pleasure. Who would have guessed? That night the two guys continued to cuddle with me and caress my body. Yes, Sheldon did screw me one more time that night before leaving.

Many times in the days and months since that first night my husband and I have talked about how that experience launched us into the MFM lifestyle. Mel repeatedly tells me he loves watching me being pleasured by another guy as he holds me in his arms, kisses me, and whispers his love into my ear.

Memories of that night, the later one with Reggie, and similar MFM play with other guys are always fodder for great sex between Mel and me when we are alone. Mel never fails to pleasure me when we are alone together, but we have learned that periodic MFM play adds substantial spice to our shared sex life. It goes without saying that I enjoy the variety and doubled pleasure. I think I have become a much more sensual woman since we launched our new lifestyle.

Joan, you may wonder how I am able to remember all the conversations and details of our adventures that now date two years back. Two days after our evening with Sheldon my husband left town on a three-day business trip. I was left home alone with our son. I took advantage of those evenings to start a diary of our new adventures in a private portion of my computer. I guess I sensed that the sex life I shared with my husband had entered a bold new phase, and I wanted to record my memories.

Writing my "diary" was actually a "hot" experience, reflecting in words the things my husband had introduced me to. I was eager to record every detail I could remember. I may have taken some liberties with the dialog I recorded, but it certainly reflects my memory of what were then recent events.

Over the past two years I have added more memories to my diary about our continuing adventures, but I am limiting this letter primarily to how we got started in MFM play.

Oh yes, about our night with Reggie. Three weeks after our night with Sheldon, Mel invited Reggie to join him in giving me pleasure. The start was similar, but that time I was far less nervous. That night it was Mel who gave me my first oral pleasures. As he did that I played with Reggie's penis, stroking him as he sucked my breasts... and eventually taking his penis into my mouth (my first blow job for any guy other that Mel... since our marriage).

Reggie really got hard during my ministrations. I even played with his nuts as I sucked him. He seemed quite appreciative. He demonstrated his appreciation later when he screwed me continuously for more than thirty minutes before finally draining his nut sack within my vagina. Mel told me later that my pussy was overflowing with Reggie's "lubricant" when he entered me right after Reggie pulled out.

That time my libido was so sated that I did not climax as Mel took his pleasure. But, once again, our three-way play did not end after each of us had our first climaxes. As a matter of fact, since our son was staying two nights with his grandparents, and Reggie had no other plans... we invited him to spend the night with us.

I enjoyed lots more kisses, breast play, cuddling and screwing before the three of us fell asleep in our shared bed that night. My husband woke me once, lying atop me, as I felt his penis slide into me for a quickie an hour or so after I fell asleep. As he "did me" he again whispered his love for me while Reggie slept soundly beside us.

Reggie was the first to wake. I was cuddled against my husband and I felt Reggie enter me from behind. His arm was over my side and he was fondling one of my breasts as I fully awoke. It felt good to be cuddling with my husband while Reggie was slowly screwing me from behind.

Reggie continued his play within me for quite some time. When I finally reached my sweet spot (peak of my climax) my body was moving around so much that Mel finally woke up. When he was fully awake he realized that in spite of the orgasm I had just had... Reggie was still pumping within me. Mel kissed me deeply put his arm around me and hugged me tightly.

The three of us stayed like that (Reggie still playing inside me... me still enjoying it... Mel still kissing and hugging me) until I finally felt Reggie's pace increase. He unloaded inside of me as I gasped and moaned into my husband's ear. When he was totally drained, Reggie just stayed connected to me, penis amazingly still hard. He fell asleep again, against my back.

A couple hours later I managed to wiggle out from between Mel and Reggie. I took a refreshing shower, put my lace gown on, and then went down to make coffee for us. The aroma must have awakened the guys. They came down wearing only their under briefs. After breakfast the guys got me back in bed for some more play. By then I was quite at ease being the center of erotic play with two guys. My inhibitions had pretty much evaporated.

In the months that have followed we have had both Sheldon and Reggie back for three-way play... and Mel has found a few more new guys for me to experience. Each one has (in some way) been different. I have enjoyed all of them. Other than with Reggie and Sheldon, we have rented a motel room for our play. On those nights we usually just get a babysitter for our son.

By the way, when I reference "three-way play", I don't mean to imply that Mel gets into any guy-guy sex. He is hetero... strictly hetero. I am (happily) the exclusive center of attention when we invite another guy to play with us.

Joan, I have to admit that I am really happy that my husband tricked or fooled me into experiencing sex play with other guys. I have since read some of your reports, and am happy to find so many other wives whose husbands have made it possible for them to experience the variety and intense pleasure associated with MFM play.

Over the two years since Mel "tricked" me, we have had MFM adventures roughly every four to six weeks... enough to keep the sex life between Mel and me at a high level. In addition to Reggie and Sheldon, I have experienced five other new guys. Neither Mel nor I have any desire to go back to my old "no other guys" days.

The End

Here is a sample from another story you may enjoy:

JOAN VEGAS

THE MORE, THE MERRIER

FOUR WOMEN REPORT ON HAVING TWO (OR MORE) HUSBANDS

THREESOME-AWESOME SEX

Joe and I had been married for a fairly short time when we met Marv. We had bought an old house and neither Joe nor I knew much about fixing up the place.

Home Depot helped by giving lessons on different things but we constantly ran into problems with things we hadn't had experience with.

Luckily Marv, a friend of Joe's from work, offered to help. He is older, maybe 30, and a nice guy. Joe was 24 at the time, and I was 22. Marv was in a troubled marriage, and would sometime stay at our house on weekends. We all got along fine.

I would tease and flirt with him, not thinking anything of it. After all, we were just friends. One night he showed up devastated, saying his wife had left him. He was crying. She had taken their kids and moved back to Missouri with some guy she had met.

He was so broken up that although Joe tried to comfort him, it was clumsy. I took him and held him, letting him cry. It was heartbreaking to hear his wracking sobs and his body shaking with grief.

At the time our little one bedroom home had very few furnishings. In the living room we just had a TV and four frameless futons to sit on. When Marv arrived that night we were already in bed. Hearing the doorbell ring, Joe and I just put our robes on to see who it was. Mine was just a short robe, and (like Joe) I had nothing on underneath as we answered the door.

I was sitting on one of our futons in our living room, leaning against the wall when I called Marv over to me so I could console him. He sat down next to me. I was holding him tight, patting his back, cuddling him against me, and saying dumb things to him. I'm not sure when it happened, but one moment he was sobbing on my shoulder, then the next he was kissing me. I was too shocked to react.

I looked up at Joe only to find that he was smiling and mouthing the words "It's OK… comfort him."

Soon Marv's head was in my lap with his body and legs stretched out on the futon. That's when I noticed the top two buttons on my robe had come undone, and my robe was gaping open. I noticed that Marv was looking at my bare boobs, but my arms were trapped under him so I couldn't move to cover myself.

As I continued to cradle Marv in my arms, I felt him pull himself up to give me another kiss. As he did that he placed one of his hands on my nearest breast and began to fondle it. I started to pull away when I heard Joe say, "Hon, let him play. That will help him relax and forget his troubles." I was a bit bewildered at my husband's words, but I stopped pulling away and let Marv play with my breasts. Soon he was kissing one while playing with my other one… and I was just letting him. When I looked over at my husband I found that he was just grinning… obviously not unhappy about what Marv was doing with me… his wife.

Marv had stopped crying and was clearly enjoying himself in my arms as he alternately sucked my breasts. I knew my husband had sat down on one of the other futons and was watching. While still cradling Marv in my arms, boobs exposed to his play, I again looked over at my husband. He whispered, "He needs this, Hon. Go ahead."

I wasn't quite sure what "Go ahead" meant. By then, my back had slipped away from the wall and my head had settled back on one of the other futons. As Marv continued to feast on my boobs I began to feel at ease with my mother-like role of letting him suckle me while I comforted him. Besides, it felt good to feel the hands and mouth of another man playing on my body.

I saw my husband move over by my feet. My lower body was lying flat with Marv's head and shoulder at about my waist level.

I felt my husband undo the one remaining button on the lower portion of my short robe. Then he nudged my legs apart. He crawled between my legs and planted his face against my crotch.

With Marv still gently sucking one of my breasts, I felt Joe's tongue begin to flutter over my clit. What a sensation... two men playing with different parts of my body. I was getting turned-on.

Then I felt my husband's tongue dip inside my pussy. I love it when he does that... and it felt especially good that night, in that setting, with Marv's mouth sucking my nipple. I felt my body begin to involuntarily twist and buck a bit against my husband's face. I think I also hugged Marv more tightly against my chest... unintentionally encouraging him to suck harder on me. With his hand he cupped my other breast before squeezing that nipple...

If you enjoyed this sample then look for **The More, The Merrier.**

Also by this Author

About the Author

Joan Vegas was born in 1973 and grew up in a small town in mid-USA.

After graduating from college, she met two guys. Both were really special and she fell in love with both of them. She was fortunate that they love her so much. They then decided to "share" her. The three of them moved in together, later on forming a "family partnership". They eventually had four children together (the story behind it is very interesting).

Because of their unique three-way partnership family, she has gotten to know other couples where a third person was regularly a part of their intimate relationships. It is the correspondence to/from these other advocates of three-way intimacy relationships that Joan's true reports are based on. And yes, it can happen... It can be very fun, intimate, and wonderful!

"Thank you for reading my stories/reports. If you are part of a three-way intimate relationship, I would love to hear from you." -Joan-

From the Author

Check my page on Amazon and my blog for Updates and interesting info.

Author Central Page - http://amzn.to/14ZEmfs
Author Blog - http://joan-vegas.awesomeauthors.org/

If you enjoyed any of my books then please share the love and click like on my books in Amazon.

If you write me a review and send me an email I will send you a free book, or many. (Just know that these emails are filtered by my publisher.)

Good news is always welcome.

One Last Thing, For Kindle Readers...

When you turn the page, Kindle will give you the opportunity to rate this book and share your thoughts on Facebook and Twitter. If you enjoyed my writings, would you please take a few seconds to let your friends know about it? Because... when they enjoy they will be grateful to you and so will I.

Thank You!

Joan Vegas
joan_vegas@awesomeauthors.org